Mister

one-green

one-blue

To Loretta and Herb,
for encouraging me to imagine things.   – D.K.

With love to David and my family.   – S.M.

Book design by Laura Lovett.
Typeset in Berliner Grotesk and Block Berthold.
The artwork in this book was rendered in watercolor and gouache.
Printed in Hong Kong.

Library of Congress Cataloging-in-Publication Data

Keller, Debra, 1958-
        The trouble with Mister/words by Debra Keller; pictures by Shannon McNeill.
        32 p.   21.5 x 26.7 cm.
        Summary: Alex's parents think a dog is too much trouble, so Alex finds another way
            to have the dog he's always wanted.
        ISBN 0-8118-0358-9
        [1. Dogs–Fiction. 2. Imaginary playmates–Fiction.]
        I. McNeill, Shannon, 1970-   ill.   II. Title.
        PZ7.K281315Tr 1995
        [E]–dc20   94-4048
                                                          CIP
                                                            AC

Distributed in Canada by Raincoast Books
8680 Cambie Street, Vancouver, B.C. V6P 6M9

10 9 8 7 6 5 4 3 2 1

Chronicle Books
275 Fifth Street
San Francisco, California 94103

The Trouble with Mister

Words by Debra Keller

Pictures by Shannon McNeill

Chronicle Books ❋ San Francisco

There was only one thing Alex wanted in the whole wide world, and he asked for it at every opportunity.

When Alex's mother said, "What do you want in your lunchbox, sweetie?" Alex said, "A dog."

When Alex's father said, "What do you want to wear today, partner?" Alex said, "A dog."

When Alex's sister said, "What do you want to play with, Alex?" Alex said, "A dog."

"A dog is too much trouble!" they said, but Alex kept asking anyway.

One rainy afternoon Alex went to his room. There he
painted the dog he dreamed of.

Alex painted his dog as tall as himself so that he had
someone his size to play with. He gave his dog long purple
hair because he loved the taste of grape juice. He gave his
dog one green eye and one blue eye because he could not
choose between them. And to keep his dog warm in the
winter, Alex painted bright yellow socks on all four paws.

Alex showed his painting to his mother. "What a lovely horse," she said.

"It is my dog," said Alex.

Alex showed his painting to his father. "That is quite a beast," he said.

"It is my dog," said Alex.

Alex showed his painting to his sister. "Nice dog," she said.

"His name is Mister," said Alex.

Alex folded Mister over and over until he was pocket size. In school, Mister lay in Alex's backpack. On the playground, Mister snuggled in Alex's jacket. At home, Mister slept under Alex's pillow and chased bad dreams away. Alex's life was perfect.

Until Tuesday.

On Tuesday night, Alex went to bed like he always did, but he did not fall asleep.

He turned to the left. He turned to the right. He lay on his back. He flopped on his belly. Alex could not get comfortable. His pillow was too lumpy.

Alex's sister went to bed. His mother went to bed. His father went to bed. Quiet filled the house. And Alex's pillow grew lumpier and lumpier. Then it began to breathe!

Mister

"**AAAGGH!**" gasped Alex as he jumped out of bed.

"**RUMMFFF,**" mumbled something near him.

Alex quickly turned on the light, and who should pop out from under his pillow but Mister!

Mister was not flat and folded the way Alex put him to bed. Now he was as tall as Alex and twice as round. He wagged his purple tail, blinked his green and blue eyes, and shuffled in his bright yellow socks.

Alex led Mister to the living room where his parents would not hear them. Then Alex said, "Mister, shake hands!" Mister raised his paw.

Alex said, "Mister, sit!" Mister sat.

Alex said "Mister, lie down!" Mister lay flat.

Alex said, "Mister, roll over!" Mister rolled. Alex hugged Mister tightly and said, "What a good dog, Mister! You are no trouble at all!"

Alex and Mister romped and rolled and fetched and tugged. They rested for a little while and then they played some more. When the moon sunk low and the sky got light they tiptoed upstairs to bed.

With a wiggle and squiggle and a great big **HUMPH,** Mister tucked himself under Alex's pillow and they both fell fast asleep.

But not for long.

Alex woke up with a jolt. His father, his mother,
and his sister were all towering over his bed.

"The house is in ruins."

"Everything's broken."

"Explain yourself!" they said.

"It wasn't me," said Alex. "It was Mister! Look!" He whipped his pillow off his bed. But there was nothing underneath it.

"Mister! Hey, Mister!" Alex called, but Mister did not answer. Alex looked in his closet. He looked in his toy chest. He looked under his bed. Mister was not there.

Alex looked upstairs. He looked downstairs. He looked outside. Mister was nowhere.

Alex phoned the humane society. "Sorry, no long haired purple dogs here," a man said.

Alex put an ad in the newspaper: **LOST. LONG HAIRED PURPLE DOG.**

Alex painted signs and hung them on telephone poles around the neighborhood: LOST. LONG HAIRED PURPLE DOG.

LARGE REWARD. NO QUESTIONS ASKED.

A day passed. A week passed. A month passed.

Alex's family forgot all about Mister but Alex did not. With every day that Mister did not return, Alex grew more miserable.

Then one afternoon the phone rang. Alex answered it.
"Hello," said a woman. "I am calling about your lost dog.
I think I found him."

"Does he have long purple hair?" asked Alex.

"The color of grape juice," said the woman.

"Does he have one green eye and one blue eye?" asked Alex.

"I don't know which is more beautiful," said the woman.

"Is he wearing bright yellow socks?" asked Alex.

"Warm ones, on all four paws," said the woman.

"IT'S MISTER!" shouted Alex.

"I am certain it is," said the woman.

The woman agreed to bring Mister over that evening, but refused to accept a reward.

That night at the dinner table Alex sat smiling. He made up songs about mashed potatoes and peas. He hummed. He whistled.

Alex's father, his mother, and his sister all stared.

"You're happy."

"You're beaming."

"You're up to no good," they said.

"You are imagining things," said Alex. When the doorbell rang, Alex leapt out of his chair and ran to answer it. He flung the door open with a great big **WHOOSH**, only to find a small brown envelope resting on the doormat.

Inside was a pocket-size piece of paper folded over and over again. It had water stains and dog-eared corners. Alex carefully, carefully unfolded it until he was holding a painting of a long haired purple dog with one green eye, one blue eye and bright yellow socks on all four paws. Below him was scribbled this note:

Dear Alex,
I am sorry for I ran away so I would you so very much. I

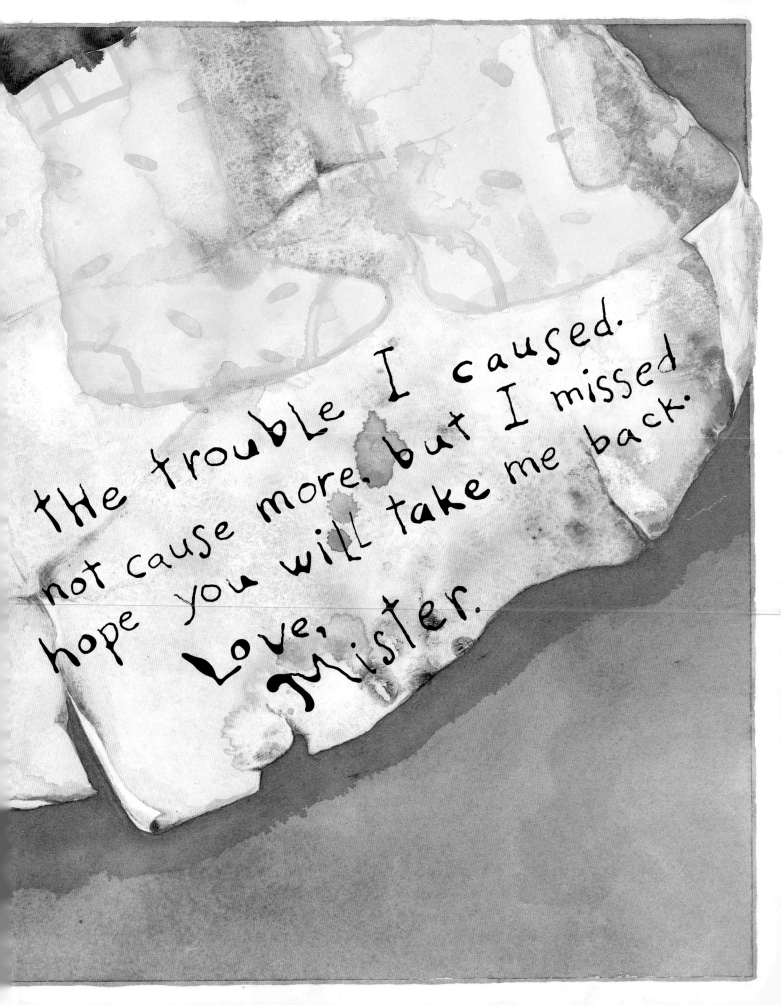

"Oh, Mister!" said Alex. He gave him a kiss. Then Alex folded Mister over and over, and put him in his shirt pocket, close to his heart.